S0-ABP-811

Hello, Maroon Tiger!

MOREHOUSE
COLLEGE

Earl Anthony Cooper
Morehouse Class of 2011

Illustrated by Chase McKesson
Morehouse Class of 2013

MASCOT® BOOKS

It was a beautiful fall day at
Morehouse College.

Maroon Tiger was on his way to
B. T. Harvey Stadium to watch
a football game.

He passed in front of Graves Hall and the
Benjamin E. Mays Memorial.

A professor waved and said,
"Hello, Maroon Tiger!"

He walked by Robert Hall
and Kilgore Hall.

A couple passing by said,
"Hello, Maroon Tiger!"

Maroon Tiger went along Brown Street.

A family sitting on one of the benches eating lunch called out, "Hello, Maroon Tiger!"

Maroon Tiger stopped by the
Martin Luther King, Jr. International Chapel.

Some students on the steps yelled,
"Hello, Maroon Tiger!"

It was almost time for the football game. As Maroon Tiger ran to the stadium, he passed by some alumni.

The alumni remembered Maroon Tiger from when they went to Morehouse College. They said, "Hello again, Maroon Tiger!"

Finally, Maroon Tiger arrived at
B.T. Harvey Stadium.

As he ran across the football field,
Morehouse fans cheered, "Let's Go, Tigers!"

Maroon Tiger watched the game from the
sidelines and cheered for the team.

Morehouse College scored six points! The quarterback shouted, "Touchdown, Tigers!"

At halftime, the House of Funk
Marching Band performed on the field.

Maroon Tiger and the crowd
sang "Dear Old Morehouse."

The Morehouse College Maroon Tigers
won the football game!

Maroon Tiger gave the Morehouse
football coach a high-five. The coach said,
"Great game, Maroon Tiger!"

After the football game, Maroon Tiger was tired. It had been a long day on the Morehouse campus.

He walked home and climbed into bed.

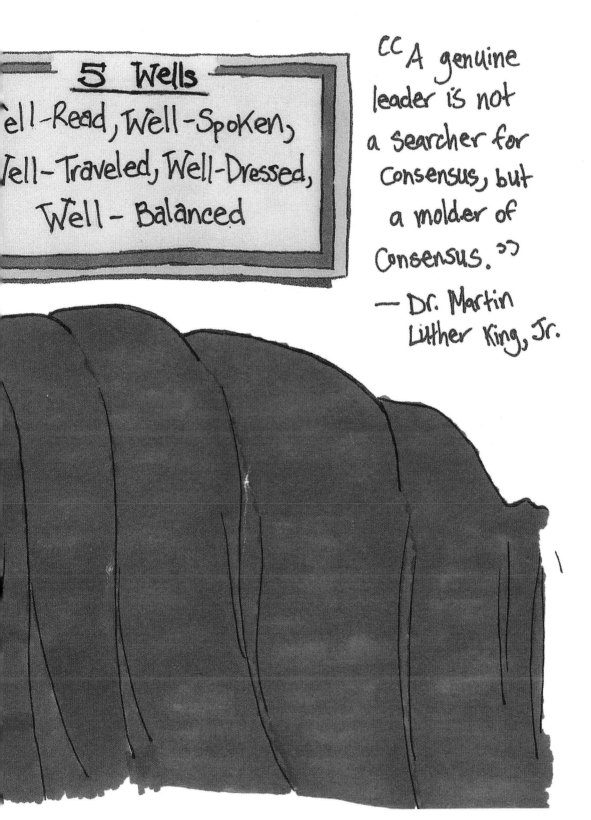

5 Wells

ell-Read, Well-Spoken,
ell-Traveled, Well-Dressed,
Well-Balanced

"A genuine leader is not a searcher for consensus, but a molder of consensus."

— Dr. Martin Luther King, Jr.

"Goodnight, Maroon Tiger."

For my family, along with all Morehouse Men who have changed the world and continue to do so. ~ EAC

For all my family and friends. Thank you so much for your constant support. I love and appreciate you all. ~ CM

Special thanks to:
"Morehouse Aunt" Susie Paige
The Mascot Books Family

MOREHOUSE

www.mascotbooks.com

Copyright © 2018, Earl Anthony Cooper. All rights reserved.
No part of this book may be reproduced by any means.

For more information, please contact Mascot Books,
620 Herndon Parkway #320 Herndon, Virginia 20170

All Morehouse College indicia are protected trademarks or registered trademarks of Morehouse College and are used under license.

ISBN 13: 978-1-936319-62-6
ISBN 10: 1-936319-62-4

PRT1217B

Printed in the United States.

About the Author

Earl is passionate about children from minority communities having the opportunity to enjoy golf. The life-changing opportunity to play golf in Wilmington, Delaware, near his home was presented to him at age six. More than a decade later, one of his proudest achievements is being one of *Golf Digest's* "Best Young Teachers in America." He has been a golf professional at Wilmington Country Club, Detroit Golf Club, and The PGA Golf Club. His passion for golf has allowed him to travel nationally and internationally. The PGA Lead program, which increases diversity in every aspect of the game, selected him as an Emerging Leader.

Earl's Historically Black College and University (HBCU) children's book series includes *Hello, Maroon Tiger!* (Morehouse College, his alma mater), *Baby Bison's First Homecoming* (Howard University), and *Good Morning, Hornet!* (Delaware State University). His series inspired the publication of *I Love My SSU* about Savannah State College and other books focusing on HBCU colleges and universities.

He is often invited to schools and community events to share his book series, his inspirational personal story, and to talk about college and life. Earl's reminder is always to *Dream Big, Because Dreams Do Come True*. For more information visit www.earlcoopergolf.com Follow him on social media @earldreambig.

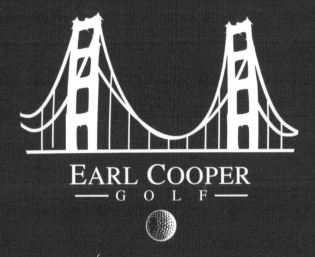

EARL COOPER
G O L F

At Earl Cooper Golf we promote access and
exposure. We're working to extend the golf greens
to all. Join us in expanding the golf umbrella. It's
big enough and sturdy enough to be inclusive
and expand opportunity, allowing anyone and all
skill levels – from duffers to pros – the chance to
experience golf's beauty, wonder, and joy, as well as
its competitiveness and camaraderie. Make it your
game. Define your experience. GO PLAY! For more
information, visit www.EarlCooperGolf.com